Stone Arch Readers are designed to provide enjoyable reading experiences, as well as opportunities to develop vocabulary, literacy skills, and comprehension. Here are a few ways to support your beginning reader:

- Talk with your child about the ideas addressed in the story.

- Discuss each illustration, mentioning the characters, where they are, and what they are doing.

- Read with expression, pointing to each word. You may want to read the whole story through and then revisit parts of the story to ensure that the meanings of words or phrases are understood.

- Talk about why the character did what he or she did and what your child would do in that situation.

- Help your child connect with characters and events in the story.

Remember, reading with your child should be fun, not forced. Each moment spent reading with your child is a priceless investment in his or her literacy life.

GAIL SAUNDERS-SMITH, PH.D.

STONE ARCH **READERS**

are published by Stone Arch Books
151 Good Counsel Drive, P.O. Box 669
Mankato, Minnesota 56002
www.stonearchbooks.com

Library of Congress
Cataloging-in-Publication Data
Meister, Cari.
   Snorp, the city monster / by Cari Meister ;
illustrated by Dennis Messner.
   p. cm. – (Stone Arch reader)
   ISBN 978-1-4342-1632-8 (library binding)
   ISBN 978-1-4342-1747-9 (paperback)
   [1. Tongue–Fiction.
   2. City and town life–Fiction.
   3. Monsters–Fiction.]
   I. Messner, Dennis, ill. II. Title.
   PZ7.M515916Sno 2010
   [E]–dc22   2009000887

Summary: Snorp has an
extra long tongue that
causes problems.

Creative Director: Heather Kindseth
Designer: Bob Lentz

Reading Consultants:
Gail Saunders-Smith, Ph.D.
Melinda Melton Crow, M.Ed.
Laurie K. Holland, Media Specialist

Printed in the United States of America

SNORP
THE CITY
MONSTER

BY CARI MEISTER

ILLUSTRATED BY
DENNIS MESSNER

STONE ARCH BOOKS
MINNEAPOLIS   SAN DIEGO

SNORP

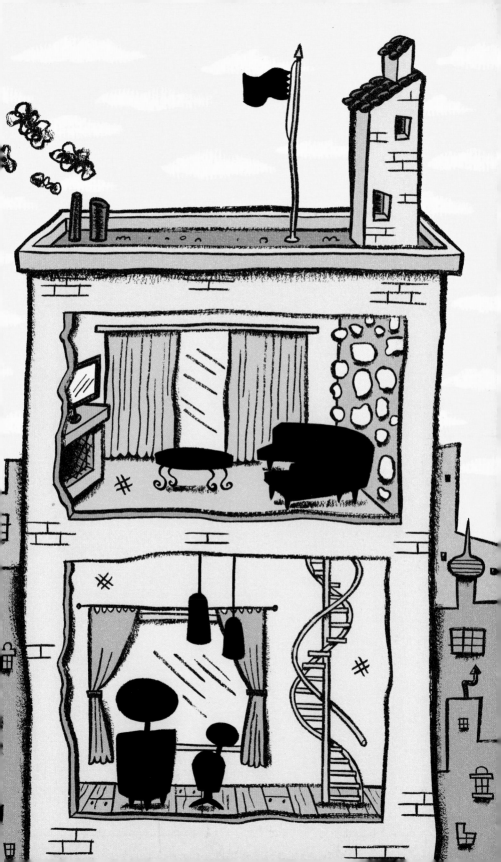

Snorp lives in the big city.
He has a very, very long tongue.

A long tongue can be useful.
Snorp is the best window washer
in town.

It is easy for Snorp to hang
his clothes to dry.

Snorp can help his friends.

Sometimes a long tongue is
a problem. Snorp's tongue does
not fit in his mouth. It drags on
the ground.

Sometimes Snorp is in a hurry. Then his tongue is an even bigger problem.

It is very hard to talk with a long tongue. No one understands what Snorp is saying.

The baker always gives him the wrong donuts.

The shoe monster always gives him the wrong shoes.

One night, Snorp asks for
ham and cheese.

The waiter brings him a hat
and sheep.

Snorp went home very hungry.

"I must do something about
my tongue!" Snorp says.

He tries wrapping it around
his head. Now he cannot see.

He tries wearing it like a belt.
Now he cannot get through the
door.

"What will I do?" Snorp says.
"My tongue will always get in
the way."

The next morning, Snorp's cousin Barker comes for a visit.

"Why are you sad?" Barker asks.

Snorp tries to answer. Barker
cannot understand him.

"I know how you feel," Barker
says.

Barker opens his briefcase.
Snorp looks inside. He sees
a tongue. It is a very, very long
tongue just like his!

"Watch," says Barker. "I learned
a trick about my tongue."

Snorp's cousin takes out the tongue.

He puts it in his mouth.

Then, he pushes his nose.

Wow! Now Barker has a long tongue too.

Barker stands on his head.
He pushes his nose again. His
tongue falls off.

He rolls it back up.

"Now you try," he says to Snorp.

Snorp stands on his head. He pushes his nose. His tongue falls off!

Snorp rolls up his tongue and puts it away. He thanks his cousin and walks to the donut shop.

Snorp tries out his short tongue.

"I will have two chocolate donuts and three glazed donuts," he says. And for the first time ever, Snorp gets the right donuts.

Now everyone understands Snorp.

And he is still the best
window washer in town.

THE END

STORY WORDS

tongue	wrapping	chocolate
clothes	cousin	glazed
donuts	briefcase	everyone

Total Word Count: 368

MEET ALL FOUR OF OUR MONSTERS!